CW01651877

**For**

**all curious children of the world !**

Manolin

# The Istanbul Adventure

By Leyla Emory & Gülsevin Kıral

Illustrations by Buket Gencer

Graphic Design by Semra Bolat

**Geese are happy little things**
**Except when coldness hits their wings.**
**They quickly flee the snowy sky,**

And towards warmer lands they fly.

In a flock, they form a V,
And glide above the deep blue sea.
It's here we find our feathered friend.
Bruce, the little goose, was at the end.

"Keep up," his mother's voice would thunder,
But Bruce's mind was full of wonder.

He saw a city sparkling **bright,**
And without thought, swooped down in **flight.**

He glided towards a glistening bay
Where a pair of street cats yapped away.

**Fatty**
**wanted his next meal,**
**But Misty,**
**she was more genteel.**

**“Give me milk,” screamed Fatty, “to fill a pool.”**
**His little mouth began to drool.**

"Shh," purred Misty, "calm down old mate."
She strutted through an imperial gate.

**Istanbul has**
**many jewels,**
**But**
## Topkapı Palace
**is the one that rules.**

**The ground on which**
**these cats now tread,**
**Is the same from**
**which the Sultans led.**

**"Five hundred years," said Misty in awe.**
**"This place was home to our ancestral paw."**

Bored, Fatty began to groom.
Suddenly, Bruce landed with a boom!

Fatty's interest was revived.
Finally, his meal arrived!
"Don't you dare," Misty said with zest,
"That is not how we treat a guest!"

But Fatty had begun to run,
So Bruce took off for other fun.

He spotted something
quite **unique.**
And decided
he should take a **peek.**

Istanbul has many a dome,
But one was two religions' home.

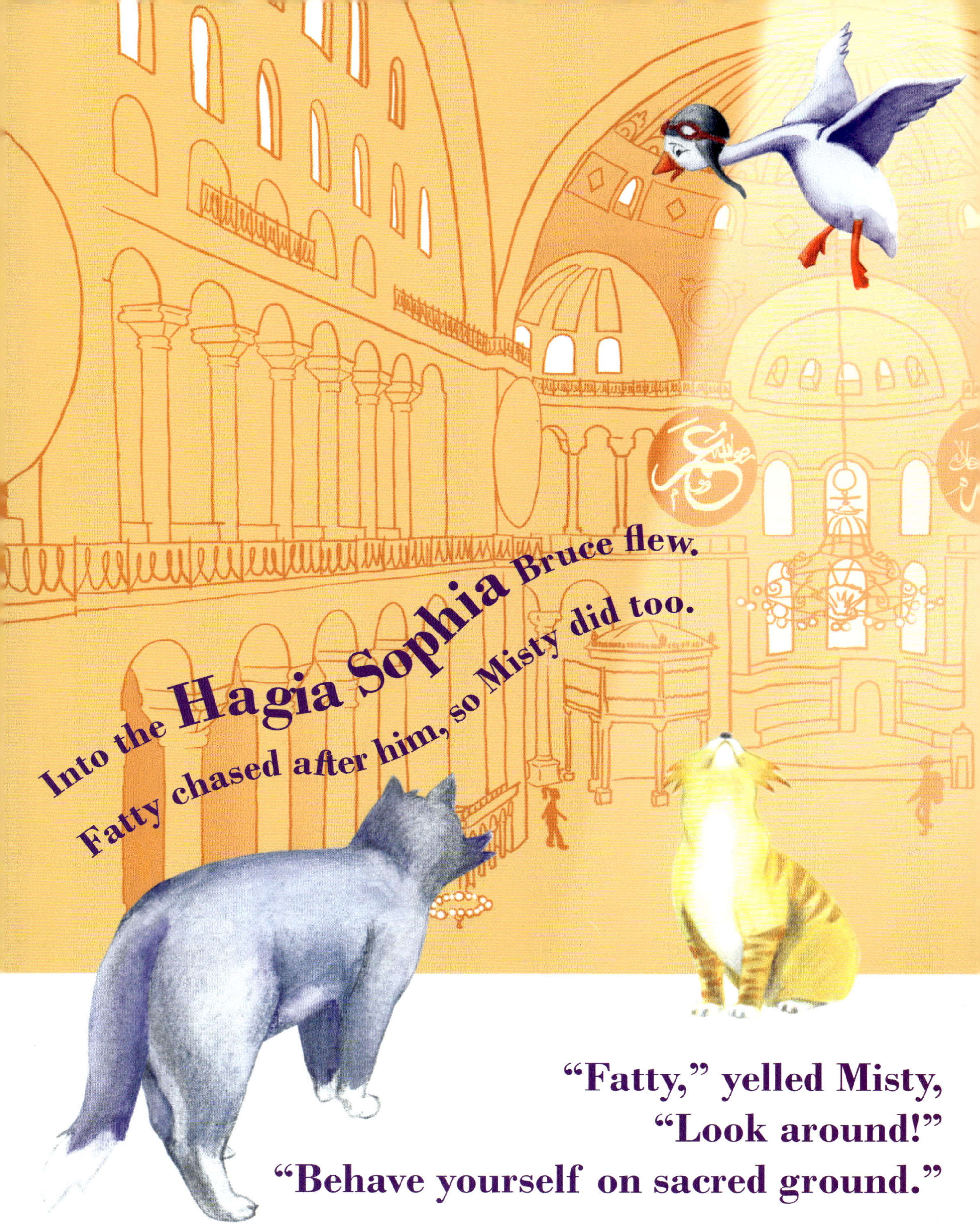

Into the **Hagia Sophia** Bruce flew.

Fatty chased after him, so Misty did too.

"Fatty," yelled Misty,
"Look around!"
"Behave yourself on sacred ground."

**"Look at the beautiful things
on the wall."
"This is no place for a silly brawl."
Bruce saw the cats lurking below,
And realized it was time to go.**

Out he flew into the sky
Where a tall structure caught his eye.
The cats ran to its base.
"Hah," Misty laughed, in Fatty's face.
"This is the **Galata Tower.**"
"Without real wings,
you have no power."

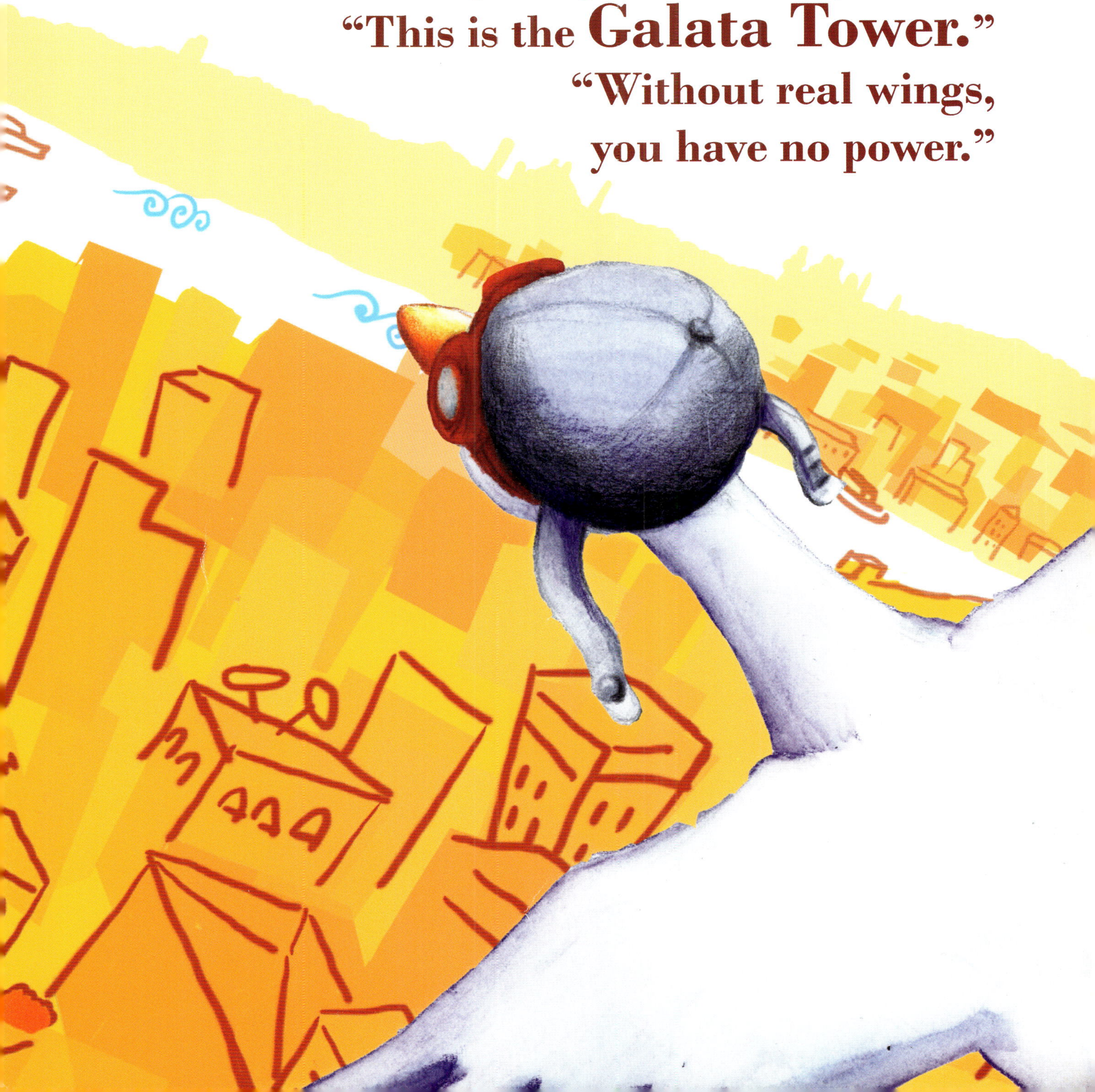

But little Bruce was tiring, too.
He needed something else to do.

Searching
for a place to dwell
He flew
inside a
massive well.

"No!"
cried Misty,
looking grim.
"Fatty,
you can not
swim!"

"The
**Basillica
Cistern**
is far too deep."
"Around its pillars,
small fish leap."

"Come," said Misty,
"dear old friend."
"Let's stroll where our
lands end."
Onto the
**Galata Bridge**
they walked,
Where for centuries,
men fished and talked.

One winked at them and slowly smiled.
In front of them four fish he piled.

They sat and ate, without a frown
Surrounded by the great old town.
A flash of white caught Fatty's eye.
Bruce was soaring through the sky.

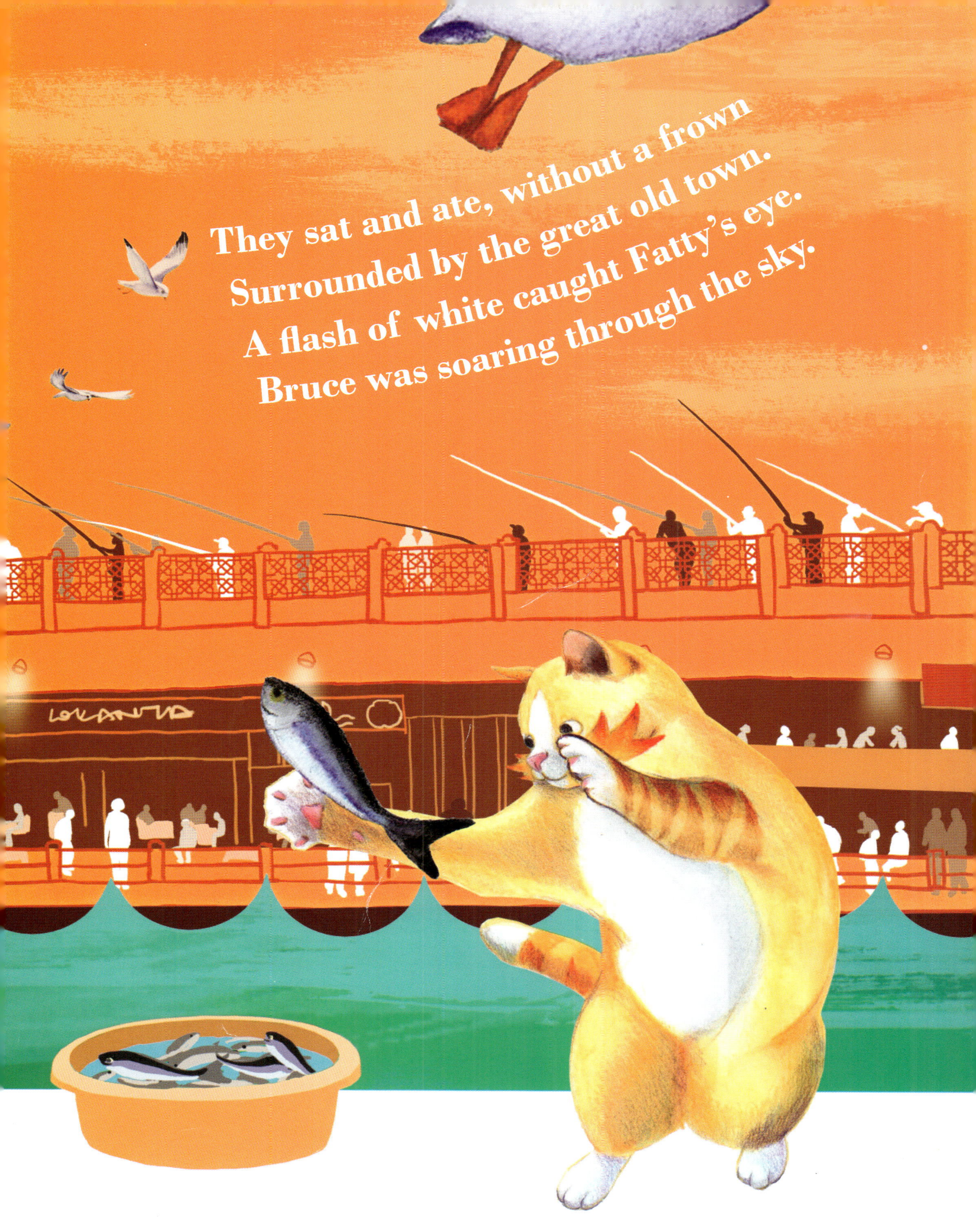

"Look," cried Fatty, "there he goes."
"Into the Grand Bazaar's wild throes."

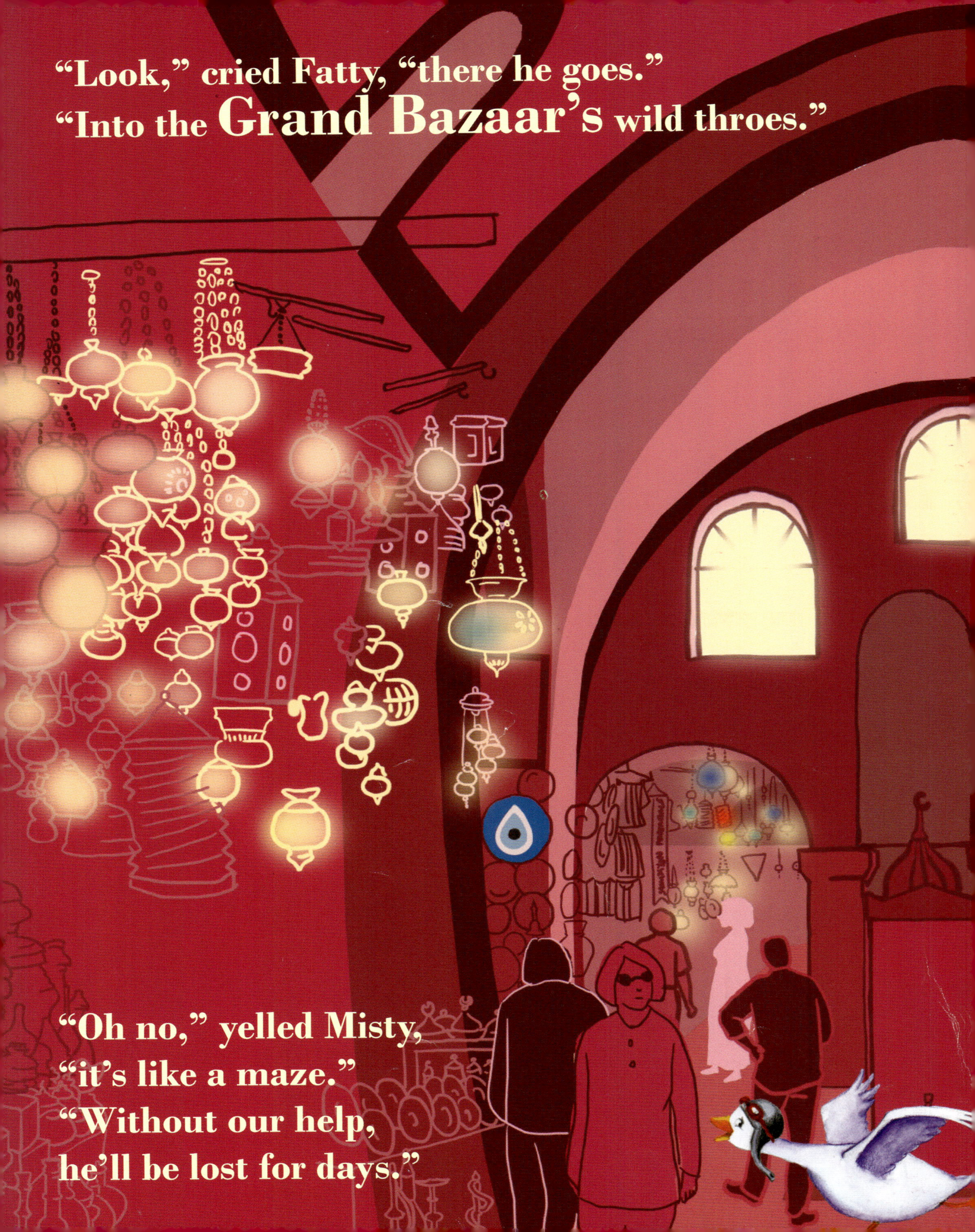

"Oh no," yelled Misty,
"it's like a maze."
"Without our help,
he'll be lost for days."

They chased Bruce through many a hall,
Until he was out of the world's oldest mall.

The cats followed Bruce's flight.
They came upon a frenzied sight.

On Taksim Square's statue, Bruce placed his feet.
He gazed at the bustle of Istiklal street.

"Little goose," yelled Fatty, his stomach now full.
"Come down and we'll show you grand, old Istanbul."
"Trying to eat you was a mistake I made."
"Accept my apologies and don't be afraid."

Taksim-Tünel

Bruce joined his guides on the ground.
Together they took in sight and sound.
Each place was better
than the last.
Each story revealed
a brilliant past.

**Dolmabahçe Palace**
was by no means the end,
But it was where Bruce
was fed by a friend.

Fatty grew jealous
and his stomach grumbled.
So towards his home
they eagerly stumbled.

**Ortaköy** is residence to many a cat.
The restaurants ensure they stay happy and fat.
With worldly tourists sat our small three
On leftover food, they dined by the sea.

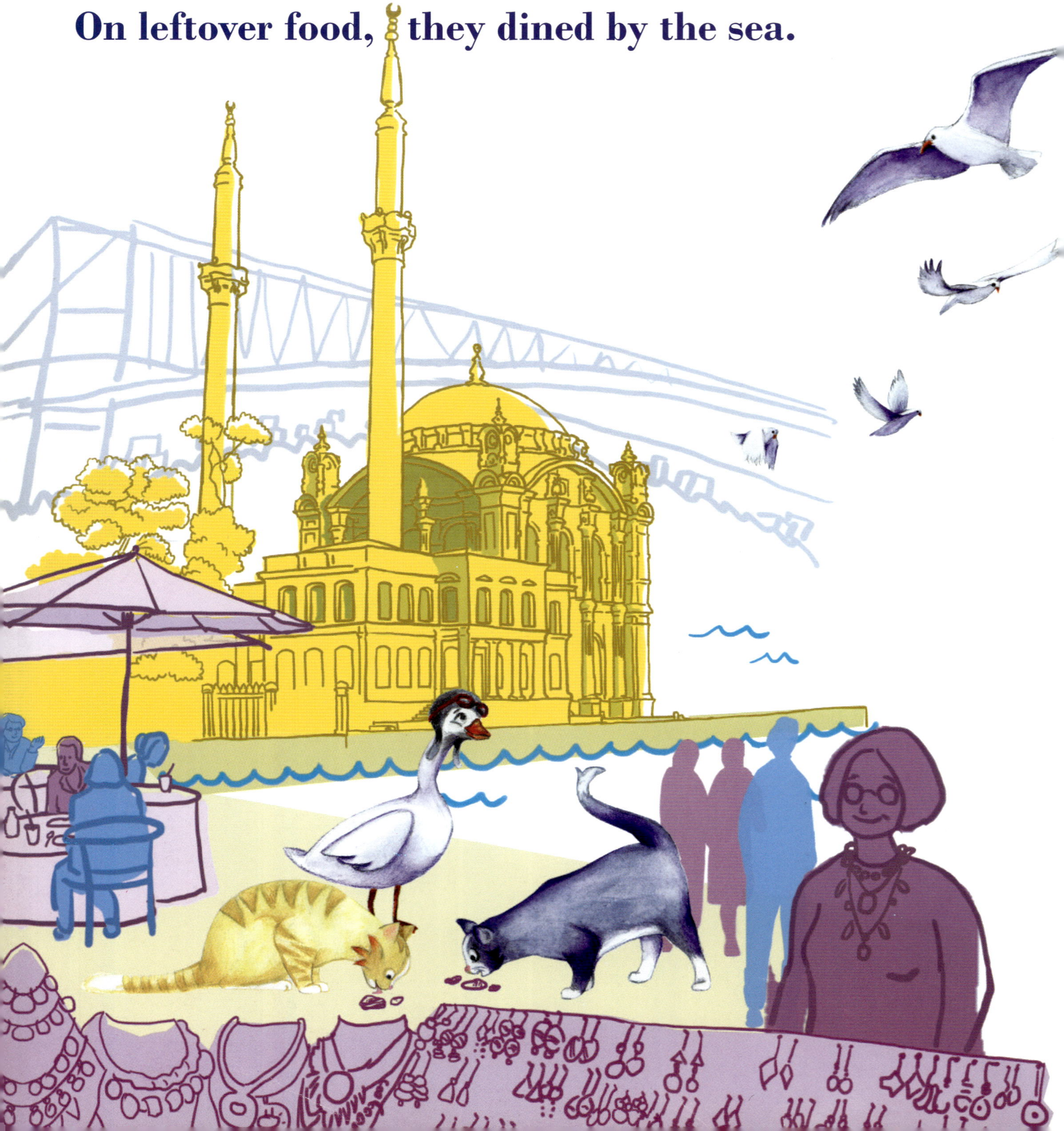

Birds flew
back and forth,
low and high
Reminding
young Bruce
of his family tie.
Spreading his
wings,
he thanked his
new friends.
Flying,
he yelled,
"I'll be back
when cold ends."
Towards
the east,
he glided away.
His heart knew
he'd be back one
day.

Meanwhile, mother goose met
with a **fright.**
Her little Bruce was no longer
in **sight.**

Towards some islands, she sharply veered.
Screeching seagulls were all that appeared.

On a tower in the sea, she searched for her kind.
Legends of maidens were all she could find.

She spotted a castle and knew right away
Her curious babe, would soon stray that way.

This mother
was right,
they rarely are wrong.
Bruce couldn’t resist,
vowing not to be long.

On the **Anatolian Fortress** he landed with glee.
His mother’s stern face, he quickly did see.

She wanted to scream, she wanted to squawk.
There’s danger in straying far from the flock,
But the joy in his eyes, she could not ignore.
Adventures are how little birds learn to soar.

**The Istanbul Adventure with Bruce the Goose**

© *2012*, Manolin
Marta Digital Publishing Ltd.

Certificate Number: 23227

*Writers* Leyla Emory & Gülsevin Kıral
*Illustrations* Buket Gencer
*Graphic Design Semra Bolat*
*Project Coordinator* Muattar Saydam

ISBN: 978-605-5311-00-1

12 13 14 15 16  9 8 7 6 5 4 3 2 1

manolin

Marta Elektronik Yayıncılık Ltd.
İSTANBUL/TURKEY
Phone : (90) 212 - 275 23 05
Fax : (90) 212 - 274 15 23
info@marta.com.tr
**www.manolinpublications.com**
www.manolin.com.tr

*Print*
**İNKILÂP KİTABEVİ BASKI TESİSLERİ**

Printer Certificate Number 10614

Sanayi Caddesi Altay Sokak No.8 Çobançeşme - Yenibosna - İstanbul
Tel.: 0 (212) 496 11 11 — Faks: 0 (212) 496 11 12
info@inkilap.com
www.inkilap.com

*All rights reserved No part of this publication may be reproduced, stored in a retrieval system or transmitted in any form or by any means, electronic, mechanical, photocopying, recording or otherwise, without the prior written permission of the copyright owner or publisher.*

**Project Sponsor**
**The Sezin School, Istanbul Turkey**
**www.sezin.k12.tr**